Curious George®

Chasing Waves

Adaptation by Alessandra Prezişi
Based on the TV series teleplay written by Justin Toly and Raye Lankford

Houghton Mifflin Harcourt
Boston   New York

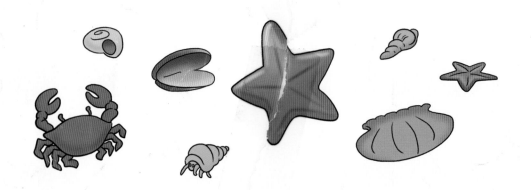

For information about permission to reproduce selections from this book, write to Permissions, Houghton Mifflin Harcourt Publishing Company, 215 Park Avenue South, New York, New York 10003.

ISBN 978-0-544-24010-0 paper over board
ISBN 978-0-544-24004-9 paperback
Design by Afsoon Razavi
www.hmhco.com
Printed in China
SCP 10 9 8 7 6 5 4 3 2 1
4500460769

George loves to travel. This weekend the man with the yellow hat took George and his friend Marco to visit Professor Wiseman at the beach.

George was excited. They got to fly in a special airplane called a floatplane. It landed on the water!

Professor Wiseman was waiting for them with a raft. George and Marco climbed aboard so the man and the professor could pull them to the beach. But George was curious. They were standing so far from the shore. Why wasn't the water deeper?

"It's low tide," Professor Wiseman explained, "and I'm standing on a sandbar. It's a big pile of sand underwater. The tide brought it in. The tide is when the gravity of the moon pulls on the ocean and makes the water come in and go out." George was amazed!

When they got to the shore, George and Marco were surprised by all of the puddles on the beach. "Those are called tidal pools," Professor Wiseman told them. "When the tide goes out some water gets left behind in holes in the sand."

There were fish, starfish, and anemones in the tidal pools. George and Marco wanted to dig for clams. Maybe if they dug deep enough, they could even find some buried treasure! They dug and dug, but buried treasure was hard to find. Maybe they should bury their own treasure! They ran up to the house to see what they could find.

Luckily, George had packed a treasure chest! Marco decided to put his favorite thing in the chest: a silver wolf necklace.

George and Marco hurried back to the beach and started digging. They made a hole and placed their treasure chest inside. Then they covered it with sand. Now they just needed a way to remember where it was buried.

George had an idea. He could measure how many steps there were between their hiding spot and the pier. The treasure was buried five giant George steps away from the third post of the pier. Now that that was done, it was time to go swimming!

"Look! A dolphin!" Marco yelled. They ran to the end of the pier to get a closer look. "Did you know that dolphins look like fish, but they're really mammals? A dolphin breathes air through a hole in the top of its head." George was surprised.

"That's right," Professor Wiseman said. "This one is friendly. His pod usually comes in with the tide. A pod is a group of dolphins that travel together."

"He looks like he wants to play," the man said. George and Marco weren't the only ones who wanted to swim!

Swimming with the dolphin was fun! He could move very fast and stay underwater for a long time—much longer than George or Marco could hold their breath.

The dolphin even found Marco's mask underwater when it fell off.

"Dolphins are excellent at finding things. They use something called sonar. He made sounds underwater and the sounds bounced off the mask and told him where to find it," Professor Wiseman said. Marco thanked the dolphin and they started swimming back to shore.

"Why can't we walk back?" Marco asked. "I thought you could touch the bottom."

"We could before, but the tide has been coming in while we've been playing. Now we have to swim," the man explained.

When they got back to the shore, George and Marco realized they had a big problem!

The tide was higher now, so the water covered more of the beach—including the spot where their treasure was buried! "Don't worry," Professor Wiseman said. "The tide will go back out in about six hours. I'm sure you'll find your treasure then."

Later that afternoon, when the tide had finally gone back out, George measured five giant steps from the third post of the pier. He and Marco started digging at the spot. But their treasure chest wasn't there.

Then Marco spotted something. "Look, George!" He pointed. "It's our treasure chest!" The tide was so powerful, it had carried their treasure down the beach.

George opened the treasure chest, but it was empty. The treasure was gone. Marco had lost his favorite thing: his silver wolf necklace. George wanted to help find it, but what if it was in the ocean? They'd never be able to find Silver Wolf way out there.

Then George remembered someone who could! If dolphins were excellent at finding things, maybe the dolphin could use sonar to find Silver Wolf.

Ta-da! In no time, the dolphin appeared with the necklace around his nose. Now George and Marco had one more treasure: a new friend.

Making Waves

George and Marco learned a lot about the tides on their trip to the beach. But you don't have to go to the ocean to see waves. You can make waves right in your own home!

You'll need:
- a clean, clear 2-liter bottle with a screw-on cap
- water
- cooking oil
- blue food coloring

First, fill the bottle 2/3 of the way with water. Add a few drops of blue food coloring to make the water look like the ocean. Next, fill the bottle up the rest of the way with oil and screw the cap on tight. Lay the bottle on its side and allow it to settle for a minute. Hold each end of the bottle and gently rock it from side to side to make waves inside your own ocean bottle!

Did You Know?

George learned that even though dolphins look like fish, they're actually mammals. Did you know that whales and manatees are mammals too? That means they breathe air, nurse their babies, and are warm-blooded. Here are some more fun facts about dolphins.

- Dolphins travel in groups called pods, usually made up of ten to twelve dolphins.
- They can swim underwater for up to 15 minutes, but they can't breathe underwater.
- A female dolphin is called a cow, a male dolphin is a bull, and a baby dolphin is called a calf.

Land or Sea?

Even though dolphins breathe air, we know that they live in the ocean. Look at the animals below. Can you pick out which animals live on land and which live in the sea?

Answers: The fish, crab, and whale live in the sea.